CW00892527

Once Upon a Loon

text and photography by Scott Rykken

Copyright © 2021 by Scott Rykken

All world rights reserved.

No part of this book may be reproduced, stored in a retrieval system, or transmitted in any form or by any means electronic, mechanical, photocopying, recording or otherwise, without the prior consent of the publisher.

Readers are encouraged to go to MissionPointPress.com to contact the author or to find information on how to buy this book in bulk at a discounted rate.

Published by Mission Point Press
2554 Chandler Rd.
Traverse City, MI 49696
(231) 421-9513

MissionPointPress.com

ISBN: 978-1-954786-60-8
Library of Congress Control Number:

Printed in the United States of America

For Rosemary, Lars, Anders, and Bennett

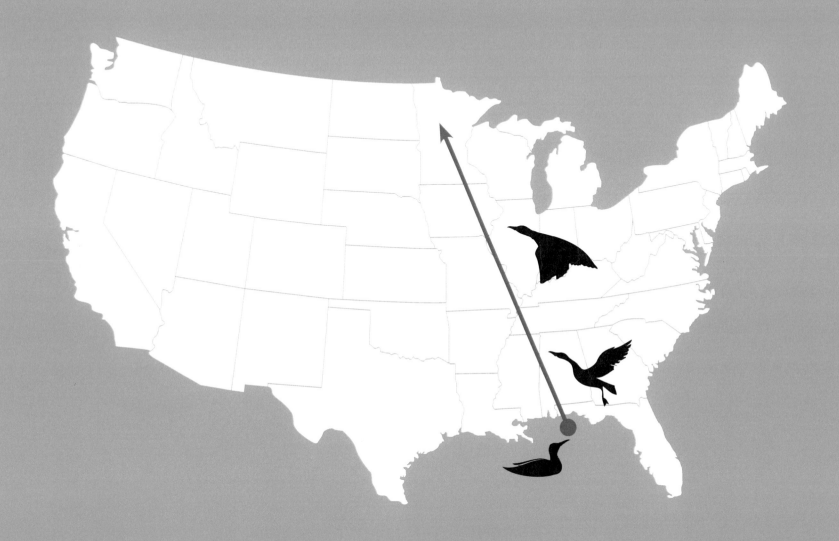

Each spring as snow and ice melt, Lucy the loon flies to Minnesota from Florida.

"It's a long ways to go," Lucy thinks to herself.

Once there, Lucy meets a mate, and together they search for the perfect place for a nest.

An island or a floating raft is ideal.

"Home sweet home."

"Ahh, isn't this lovely, dear?"

Lucy soon lays two olive-green speckled eggs, and for the next 28 days she will sit on them through all kinds of weather.

28, 27, 26, 25 . . . .

It's a lonely job being a loon mom. One day, a muskrat climbed aboard the raft. "May I join you?" asked the muskrat.

"Sure!" exclaimed Lucy. "Grab some breakfast and join me. We can talk while you eat!"

Munch, munch, munch.

Before long, another muskrat joined them.
"Nice to meet you," said Lucy.

"If you don't mind, we will hang out over here," said the muskrat.

"Sure," said Lucy. "I am just glad to have company!"

"Hi Friends!"

Once the turtles saw Lucy was friends
with the muskrats, they wanted to be friends too.

Lucy soon had many turtle friends.

One especially friendly turtle had a very important question for Lucy. "There is something I have always wanted to know," said the turtle. "What is it like to fly?"

"Try this," said Lucy. "Close your eyes. Stretch your legs out and feel the wind beneath you. That is what flying is like."

"I'm flying! I'm flying!" said the turtle.

"How does it feel?" asked Lucy.

"It is so awesome!" said the turtle.
"Thank you, friend!"

"Flying is freedom," said Lucy.
"Do you feel free?" she asked.

"I am free!" said the turtle.
"I love to fly!"

Later, Lucy asked "Perhaps you can help me. Can you watch eggs while I go for a swim and get some lunch?"

"Love to!" said the turtle.

So the turtle took turns watching
the eggs with another turtle
while Lucy took a lunch break.

"That's what friends do,"
thought the turtle.

Lucy returned and moved her eggs.
"Thank you for watching my eggs," said Lucy.

"What did you see while you were gone?" asked the turtle.

"I saw the prettiest rainbow!" said Lucy.

"I cannot see it," said the turtle sadly.

"Climb upon my back and then maybe you will be able to see it," said Lucy.

"Is that okay?" asked the turtle.

"Yes!" said Lucy. "I am happy to help a friend."

As the turtle climbed, she began to slip off.

"Let me help you," said Lucy. She reached back
and supported her friend with her wing.

Lucy, the turtle, and the muskrat sat together on the platform until the sun set. "The world is beautiful," said the turtle.

"Yes, it is," agreed the muskrat.

"Yes," said Lucy. "Especially with friends."

The next day, the first egg hatched and the baby loon was soon swimming with Mom and Dad.

"Oh, what should we name him, dear?"

"Rockabye baby, on a loon's nest."

"Where's the baby?"

"Where's the baby?"

"I thought you were watching him!"

While Mom, Dad, and the first baby were away swimming, the second egg hatched. Luckily, the turtle and all of her friends were there to help keep the new baby loon company.

"I'm coming! I'm coming!"

Eventually the loon baby heard Mom and Dad out beyond the reeds and bravely swam out to join them.
"Will you be back?" called out the turtle to Lucy.
"Not until next spring," said Lucy. "The raft is all yours!"

"Life is good, especially with friends," thought Lucy.

Loon Story

During the past three springs, we have put out a floating platform in hopes of attracting nesting loons. The platform goes out as soon as the ice melts.

Loons typically lay two large olive-green speckled eggs. We have observed that the female does most of the nest sitting while the male patrols, watching for threats and sounding an alarm whenever one appears. The eggs hatch approximately 28 days after being laid, and the chicks go to the water within 24 hours, never to return to the nest. For the first few weeks, they will ride and rest on their parents' backs. The babies are voracious eaters, and both parents work diligently to feed them. While the babies grow very rapidly, they are susceptible to a variety of threats: birds of prey (especially eagles), large fish (especially muskies or northern pikes), and even attacks from other loons, which means usually only one chick will survive the summer. At the end of the summer, the parents will fly separately to the southern US, usually along the coasts, and the remaining first-year children will join together into flocks which fly south a month later than their parents.

Loons do not necessarily mate for life, but do seem to return to the same lake the next spring. We have had successful nesting from our loons during all three springs. Loons who successfully nest will usually return the next year, and we are pretty sure the same female has returned each year.

This spring brought new sights to our loon platform. Muskrats decided to share the corner of the platform with the nesting loon. While she kept a close eye on them, she did not seem to be bothered by their presence either. As muskrats mostly eat vegetation, they did not appear to be any threat to the loon or the eggs. Turtles have also always been a part of the crowd on the platform, sunning themselves alongside the nesting loon. The most unusual sight was on the day we watched a painted turtle slowly climb upon the loon. Again, she did not seem bothered by the turtle's contact, nor did she make any attempt to get the turtle off her back. We watched this unfold over a thirty-minute period. The results are documented by this story.

"What a great story, eh, Lucy?"

About the Author and Photographer

Scott Rykken, a lifelong Minnesotan currently residing in Saint Paul, retired from teaching high school science after thirty-seven years. He currently spends his time exploring his other passions of nature and landscape photography, hiking, cross-country skiing, biking, and traveling. He was inspired to create this children's book after a series of photos he took while watching a loon family at the family cabin in Miltona, Minnesota. Parents of grown children, Scott and his wife Anne also spend much of their time doting on their four inquisitive, nature-loving grandchildren.

Lightning Source UK Ltd.
Milton Keynes UK
UKRC030105160223
417099UK00020B/284